God's Transmitters

GOD'S TRANSMITTERS

HANNAH HURNARD

Tyndale House Publishers, Inc.
Wheaton, Illinois

Library of Congress Catalog Card Number 75-13946
ISBN 0-8423-1085-1, paper
United States publications rights
secured by Tyndale House Publishers, Inc.,
Wheaton, Illinois 60187.
Published with the permission of
The Church's Ministry Among the Jews (Olive Press),
London, England.
American edition copyright © 1978 by
Tyndale House Publishers, Inc.
Reset and reissued, August 1986
Printed in the United States of America

95   94   93   92
24   23   22   21

Contents

Chapter 1	The Problem of Ineffective Prayer	7
Chapter 2	God's Transmitters	13
Chapter 3	Faith	35
Chapter 4	Love	49
Chapter 5	Answers to Some Queries	71

CHAPTER 1
The Problem of Ineffective Prayer

This little book is especially meant for prayer groups and individual Christians who are sorrowfully conscious of a strange powerlessness in their prayer life. A sense of unreality in prayer and lack of results is a real problem to many people in many parts of the world.

There may sometimes be much zeal in Christian service and witness, joy in church fellowship, generosity in giving to the

Lord's work, a great longing for the salvation of souls, and yet, with it all, one startling and challenging fact emerges, that many of the Lord's people in every part of the world are drearily conscious of something vitally wrong with their prayer life.

Though they long to be intercessors uniting with their Lord in his prayers at this time of tremendous crisis in the world's history, and to hasten the coming of his kingdom, they are almost in despair over their inability to intercede, or even to spend more than a few moments each day in prayer. Even those few minutes seem to them to be futile and powerless in the extreme, without anything really vital being accomplished.

Sometimes people say so earnestly and eagerly, "I do want to help God's work in some way. Tell me what I can do." And then, when the answer is given, "Will you join the army of intercessors and really pray?" the eager, happy look dies away, while those who are too honest to answer glibly, "Yes, I will certainly pray, that is one thing I know I can do to help," stand silent, and the wistful or pained expression on their faces says as plainly as possible, "I am really sorry; I feel that my money or some other gift might possibly be used to help, but not my prayers. If anyone really wants help and succour and power through my prayers, I am dreadfully afraid they will accomplish nothing. I wish I knew the secret of power in prayer, but I do not."

Again, in personal conversation with truly earnest Christians, the same deep longing for more reality and power in prayer is often expressed in some such words as these: "I am so troubled about my prayer life. I have a list of names of people for whom I feel I ought to pray, or who have definitely asked me to pray for them. And this list seems to grow longer and longer, until it is becoming such a dull and dreary burden that I really dread my prayer times. And worse still, I begin to wonder if going through the list conscientiously every day, and asking God to bless or help each one named, has any real effect at all.

"Is it really what he means by prayer? For doesn't he know far better than I do just what each one needs, and am I really to suppose that he will not give them what they need if I stop asking him to do so?

"What do you think intercession really means? and how can I make my prayers for others more effective, and not just a tiring, almost irksome duty which my conscience will not let me shirk? As for being a real intercessor, which I suppose means wrestling in prayer for others, I just don't seem able to do that at all. In any case, even if I knew how to do it, I could never find the time to wrestle in prayer daily for all those on my prayer list as well as for the mission fields around the world. And, once more, can it really be possible that God will withhold his help and blessing from those who need him, just because many of us fail to ask him to do so?"

Oh, how often I myself have been bewildered and troubled at my own reactions, and feelings and questionings during some prayer meetings asking myself in utter perplexity, "Is this prayer meeting really in contact with God's power and can anything vital and terrific result from it? Here we are spending it in the accustomed way, with two or three people offering long prayers in pious phraseology, reminding God of a list of things he knows already, and suggesting what we would like him to do; while everyone else feels that they have done their part by adding Amen at the end?"

Sometimes with a kind of horrified shock I have thought, "Would we really behave at all like this, or even dare to speak to him in this way, if, all of a sudden we really saw him standing in our midst, alive and present with us and expecting us to pray, and to cooperate with him in his plans for winning the world to himself?"

I know of course that the reason why many earnest Christians simply cannot attend services where the prayers are extempore is that such prayer seems to them so irreverent and lacking in a vital sense of the reality of God's presence. But then, many other equally earnest and devout Christians find just the same unreality in formal, though beautifully worded litanies and intercessions. We are all so different, we must remember that what is real and helpful to one person is not so to another. So we must not judge one another.

But when he stands amongst us in our prayer meetings or prayer groups, listening to our voices talking on and on, and looks into our minds when our heads are bowed and sees our wandering or dreary thoughts; or when we kneel before him in our times of private prayer, with what Evelyn Underhill once dubbed our celestial shopping lists, or prayer lists, open before us, may it not be that over and over again he wonders that there is no intercessor?

Is not the very fact that, generally, the weekly prayer meeting in a church is, with few exceptions, the smallest and most ill-attended meeting in the week, a dreadful proof, if we will but face it, that something has gone tragically wrong with our whole conception of what a prayer meeting really ought to be, or at least in our actual practice of it. We put the blame on the people who don't come to the prayer meeting and say they are cold and unspiritual Christians, but perhaps they are quite right in thinking that there is little use in their going to such a meeting.

It may well be that our Lord is longing to help us to a new discovery, or rather re-discovery of an entirely different and gloriously powerful ministry, through prayer and intercession, and wonders why we are so slow and unwilling to be shown it!

Perhaps the long-prayed-for-revival throughout the whole Church waits for the time when God's people enter radiantly and thankfully, yes, and adventurously, into this glorious ministry of intercession; not as a burdensome duty but as the most joyfully creative and inspiring part of their Christian life and service.

CHAPTER 2

God's Transmitters

"I sought for a man amongst them . . . that should stand in the gap before me for the land, that I should not destroy it, but I found none" (Ezek. 22:30).

"And he saw that there was no man, and wondered that there was no intercessor" (Isa. 59:16).

It seems, then, that in our generation, all around the world, many of God's people are longing, with an ever deepening intensity, for power in prayer, and seeking to understand how they may experience and practice this greatest possible privilege and delight, which the sons and daughters of God are meant to possess in Jesus Christ, the ministry of intercession. How many of us yearn to live actually in the realm of love, to be at home, in the heavenly places, instead of having to strain painfully and wearily, as it were standing on tip toe, in order to enjoy for a few moments an experience which we know ought to be habitual to the children of God! Wondering why we have to wrestle and labor to attain it, instead of finding it as natural and spontaneous, and almost as effortless, as bodily breathing.

What, then, does the Bible really mean by intercession?

There are two special verses in the Old Testament which seem to answer this question, and which are confirmed by our Lord's own example and teaching.

Ezekiel lived in a generation when the chosen people of God had become so utterly apostate that they had lost all reality in their worship, being completely materialistic and blind to spiritual truth. The picture painted by God himself through the prophet, of those evil times, is terrible in its vividness. (Ezekiel 22, 24-29):

"A conspiracy of the prophets in the midst thereof."

"The priests have violated my law."

"Like a roaring lion ravening the prey, the prophets have devoured souls."

". . . Princes like wolves . . . ravening to shed blood, and to destroy souls and to get dishonest gain."

"The people of the land use oppression . . . exercise robbery . . . vex the poor and needy."

One could imagine, apart from the difference in language and expression, that these were headlines from one of our own daily papers. The same frightful violence and crime and oppression and corruption are common in Christianized countries in our day. Looking out on this situation, and drawing the attention of his servant the prophet to these glaring headlines, God is reported as speaking thus:

"And I sought for a man amongst them that should make up the hedge and stand in the gap before me for the land, but I found none" (v. 30).

In Isaiah 59 we have another picture, equally graphic, of the same kind of situation, hands defiled with blood and feet that run to do evil. "They conceive mischief—and bring forth iniquity." "In transgression and lying against the Lord, and departing away from our God, speaking oppression and revolt, conceiving and uttering from the heart words of falsehood; judgment is turned away backward, justice standeth afar off, truth is fallen in the street . . . and he who seeks to depart from evil is accounted mad" (margin v. 15).

Then Isaiah stops, as it were, reading out the awful headlines describing the situation in his beloved country, and says, with what sounds very like horrified sorrow, "And the Lord saw it, and he saw that there was no man, and wondered that there was no intercessor" (Isa. 59:16). "No intercessor!" the prophet exclaims. Notice that it is not said God wondered that there was no one he could use as a great reformer or revivalist, or deliverer. No. There were no intercessors, not even one! And that apparently was the one thing needful which would have altered the whole situation.

Surely it is significant that God revealed to both these prophets that the vital need in that desperate situation, the one thing so lacking, was intercession. To Ezekiel he said that he had looked for a man to stand in the gap, to join up a broken place in the fence. And Isaiah was told that what God looked for was an intercessor (a *maphgia* is the Hebrew word which he used), namely something or someone to bring two separate things together so that they should meet again and be in contact. From this root comes the modern Hebrew word for contact.

What did God mean when he said that he had looked to see if there was even one man whom he could use as an intercessor? Someone to be a means of contact, or conductor of power, to bridge the gap which had come in the relationship between himself and his chosen people.

Is it not a remarkable fact also, that, in the story of Abraham interceding for the wicked cities of the plain, Abraham felt that those cities should and could be saved if there were only fifty righteous persons in them. Then he reduced the number lower and lower till it reached only ten such righteous people. And God readily declared, "I will not destroy it for ten's sake." Now why should that be so?

Surely he meant that if there were even ten people in that wicked city, living in vital contact with himself, and as intercessors, the situation was not hopeless, but the city assuredly could be saved. For through them he could influence the whole wicked, corrupted population and bring about their salvation. It is an overwhelmingly challenging thought. The awful part was, however, that nothing could be done for Sodom and Gomorrah because there were not even ten people in those cities living in vital contact with God.

Even Lot himself, the one righteous or good man, was useless. Certainly he was vexing himself, so we are told, from day to day, because of the unspeakable crimes daily committed, and because of the anguish of the helpless slave population exploited and tortured by men who had become fiends. But Lot was not an intercessor. He was living, apparently, as a godly man by profession, but actually out of contact with God, and out of contact with his fellow men, and thus he could never bridge the gap and become a conductor by means of which the saving power of God could reach the people of the cities.

An intercessor means one who is in such vital contact with God and with his fellow men that he is like a live wire closing the gap between the saving power of God and the sinful men who have been cut off from that power. An intercessor is the contacting link between the source of power (the life of the Lord Jesus Christ) and the objects needing that power and life.

To me this has come as a completely new and staggering realization. The truth seems to be that God has chosen us, in Christ Jesus (as it were, plugged into the life of Christ), to be transmitters of his life and power and love to others. Christians are a vital necessity in the world because when united with their Lord and Savior Jesus Christ and with their fellow men, they are literally the means by which God can, and does, reach the minds and wills of those who are cut off from all personal contact with Him themselves. We are called to be God's transmitters, through whom he can transmit his creative, redemptive, saving power to the minds of other people.

It is stupendous! If we are in vital contact with God in Christ, and also in contact with our fellow men through love, whenever our thoughts and minds are completely controlled by the Holy Spirit of love, then, without effort or struggle on our part, we are what God has always intended us to be, actual transmitters and conductors of his life and light and love. Our Lord and Savior Jesus Christ is the actual power house and abiding in him, that is, plugged into him by faith, we transmit his saving power to others. This was the whole typical meaning of the ministry of the priests of old: they were mediums of communication between God and men.

If we read the Bible with a clear understanding of this glorious truth, it is amazing to find how it is emphasized over and over again that it is God's purpose that every individual believer in Christ should become a transmitter of the life and thoughts of Christ. It is God's purpose for us, not only in our Christian witness and service, but perhaps especially in our private prayer life, and also in our public prayer together. It is his will that every prayer meeting should be a power house experience, when every person present should be in vital contact with God's thoughts and purposes and power, and be so controlled by the Holy Spirit (who is the holy thinker) that he can receive God's gracious thoughts into his mind and then transmit them to others, as impulses or promptings to respond to life and love of God.

Doesn't this throw a flood of almost blinding light on the real purpose and power of prayer? Think of the parable of the Importunate Widow, as it is called. It is expressly stated that our Lord told this parable in order to teach us "that men ought always to pray and not to faint" (Luke 18:1). What exactly does this mean? Why did he choose the simile of an unjust judge who must be ceaselessly importuned? For surely God is a loving heavenly Father and knoweth what things ye have need of before ye ask and does not need to be ceaselessly importuned?

Yes, certainly if we are in vital contact with God, we have indeed no need to importune him for things which he knows are needed, and which he is longing and planning to give.

But what if it is true that prayer does not mean that we importune God, but that God himself importunes others through us? God through us ceaselessly assaulting the minds of the hard and the wicked and the impenitent, as well as the minds of the sorrowful, and the broken-hearted and the anguished and the ignorant, and them that are out of the way.

Doesn't this, for some of us, completely revolutionize our idea of intercession and why God considers it so necessary? We are to receive into our thoughts his thoughts and gracious desires and then transmit those thoughts and desires to others. And doesn't the failure to understand this explain in large measure why some of us have been so tragically fruitless in our prayers and witness? We have thought our own thoughts, and, without realizing it, have transmitted them to others, instead of the saving thoughts of God. We have made our petitions in nice sounding, pious phraseology, but we have not allowed the Holy Spirit to make his petitions through us.

Indeed it is possible that at first the very suggestion that such a thing is possible may be rejected as unthinkable or just invention. But in Rom. 8:26, 27 we read, "We know not what we should pray for as we ought, but the Spirit himself maketh intercession for us with groanings that cannot be uttered. And he that searcheth the hearts knoweth what is the mind of the Spirit, because he maketh intercession for the saints, with groanings which cannot be uttered." J. B. Phillips translates this as follows: "We do not know how to pray worthily as sons of God, but his Spirit within us is actually praying for us (or through us) in those agonizing longings which never find words."

Are we not to understand by this, that when there is an agonized longing in our hearts for the salvation or deliverance of another, it is actually the Holy Spirit pouring his own desire for their salvation into our minds and thoughts, and thus forming the prayer for us? And can it be God the Father, the God of Love, whom God the Holy Spirit thus importunes? Can that be necessary? Is it not more likely to mean that he importunes the hearts and wills of those that need deliverance? More and more clearly scientists are coming to understand the extraordinary power and range of thought. Our Lord constantly and solemnly emphasized this truth in all his teaching. He definitely averred that a man's thoughts are more powerful and influential than anything else, and more far-reaching in their results. And now modern scientists are discovering how true this is, and we are challenged with the tremendous assumption that all our thoughts do go forth and touch and influence in some real way the thoughts of others, and that is why they are so important.

We are utterly wrong in supposing that our thoughts are our own private property. No! It seems terribly possible, indeed almost certain, that our minds are broadcasting stations, and that all our thoughts are being broadcast all the time, touching and influencing the thought waves of others for good or evil, just as their thought waves influence ours.

Then how vitally necessary it must be for our whole thought life to be completely under the control of the Holy Spirit, the holy thinker himself! And how readily we can now understand the Apostle's urgent exhortation that every thought should be brought into captivity to Christ! For the kingdom of God within us must be a glorious reality if we are to be saved from unseen but ever encompassing floods of evil thoughts.

In Ephesians 6:11, 12, Paul says, "I expect you have learned by now that our fight is not against any physical enemy, it is against organizations and powers that are spiritual. We are up against the unseen power that controls this dark world, and spiritual agents from the very headquarters of evil" (Phillips). When we realize that spirit is the opposite of material, I wonder if we ought to think of the spiritual realm as meaning the whole vast realm of thought; and of a spirit as one who is able to think; and of the Holy Spirit himself, as being God the holy thinker, eager and able to reproduce his own creative thoughts of love in us his creatures.

We can see then, how essential it is that our whole thought life should be brought under the control and reign of the Lord of love. It is in this realm that we exercise our free wills and become broadcasting stations for the eternal creator to use, receiving and transmitting his thoughts. Or else we are broadcasting stations for the powers of darkness.

When the kingdom of God becomes really established in our own thought realm, then we shall be out of reach of the evil influences of all the broadcasting stations of the world, the flesh and the devil. The thought waves of evil thinkers will not be able to touch us, so we shall not pick up any of their poisonous suggestions. We ought to have a great reaction of horror, disgust, and dread against every prompting to wrong thinking of any kind (and that means every thought that is antagonistic to love). Many of us have allowed ourselves to be almost fatally careless and indifferent about our thought habits, just because we have supposed that they affect no one but ourselves, and that if we have sufficient strength to refrain from expressing the unlovely ones in word or deed, then they are harmless.

We may perhaps have to see that the whole meaning of salvation is perfect deliverance from the power of evil thinking so that the whole realm of our thought life is completely annexed to the kingdom of God, and becomes an extension of heaven. For is not heaven the realm where the thoughts and purposes of the eternal God of love rule and express themselves and are allowed to become creative?

If we read the New Testament with this in mind, it is almost staggering to see how much the Lord Jesus spoke about this realm of the thoughts, and showed emphatically that all sin is in the thought realm. Re-read the Sermon on the Mount in the light of this. Transgressions and errors and iniquities are sinful thoughts which have been expressed in action but the actual sin itself is always in the thought realm. Before any transgression of the law of love is committed as a deed, it is first a thought. Either a thought conceived in our own minds, or received into them by the entrance of thoughts and ideas broadcast by others.

Christian Scientists, psychologists, those who practice auto-suggestion, and the followers of many modern cults, all emphasize the tremendous influence of mind over matter, of thought over material and physical things. Undoubtedly they are right in this. The very fact that they have concrete evidence to offer is proof that they have grasped part of a tremendous truth.

But the Christian revelation is the full truth, and where this is not realized or accepted there is one fatal flaw in any teaching on this subject. For those who seek to transmit their own thoughts, or group thoughts to others, or to help themselves by thinking and practicing good and healthy thoughts in their own minds, cannot achieve the maximum power which is possible. But the great and unspeakably glorious fact taught us by the Lord Jesus Christ is this, that when we are in him so that his life courses through us, then the Holy Spirit transforms us "by the renewing of our minds" (Rom. 12:2) and we become transmitters to others of the thoughts of God himself, his intercessors or transmitters.

The call to repentance and salvation can be summed up in the words of Isaiah, in chapter 55:7, 8: "Let the wicked forsake his way, and the unrighteous man his thoughts, and let him return unto the Lord, and He will have mercy upon him, and to our God for He will abundantly pardon. For my thoughts are not your thoughts, and my ways are not your ways, saith the Lord."

In Christ Jesus we are called to be God's transmitters, to be completely separated from all thoughts which are contrary to his thinking, so that we may transmit his thoughts to others. We do this in many ways. When we witness by mouth in the power of the Holy Spirit; and when we obey his command and preach the Gospel—in that way we broadcast God's thoughts and purposes audibly to others.

We also help to transmit the knowledge of God and of his character and love and goodness when we allow the Holy Spirit to use our bodies to perform visible acts of love and compassion and kindness and succour and justice and integrity and righteousness, etc., in a thousand practical and visible ways, which reveal the love and will of God.

But especially by means of intercession—that is by allowing the Holy Spirit to think in us his own redemptive thoughts towards others—we enable God to broadcast and transmit his thoughts to others.

Is it any wonder therefore that God has whole armies of those who are set aside in a special way for this task, freed from other kinds of service? In hospitals and sickrooms, and in lonely and isolated places, people learn to think the thoughts of God far more powerfully than when they were healthy and busy and engrossed with all the affairs of active living.

It may well be, also, that the thought waves which can most easily be picked up by other sufferers, and by lonely or terrified people, are the thought waves sent forth by those who were once in similar plight, and who have been delivered and have received the peace of God, so that their thoughts are stayed upon him even in the most difficult of all circumstances. Perhaps this kind of intercession is the most vital service of all, to be entrusted to his most experienced and honoured priests.

Our Lord said: "If ye shall ask anything in my name, I will do it" (John 14:14); but it is important to remember that all prayer in his name is prayer initiated, controlled and directed by him, not our own desires and petitions, but his desires and petitions made known to us, brought to the cognizance of our thoughts, so that we think them too. Only when we know and share in desires of our Lord Jesus Christ, can we really pray in his name, and not in our own.

Once again let us stop and ask ourselves if in our prayer meetings and in our times of private prayer we really pray in harmony with this truth? What do we transmit when we pray in the presence of others? Just our own nice sounding petitions, either haltingly, or fluently expressed, but actually in our own name, because we have just thought them ourselves? And must we not confess that sometimes they are very dull and prosy ideas and thoughts, because, as a matter of fact, we had to make a rather hurried dash to get to the prayer meeting at all, and our minds were full of other matters up to the very last moment.

And then, if we were to get a chance to pray audibly, it seemed just as well to burst into prayer at once and get it over, and feel free for the rest of the meeting, that is to say, free to let our thoughts wander somewhat, perhaps even to begin daydreaming! And so the Holy Spirit never had a chance to bring our thoughts into active cooperation with his at all. And don't we sometimes get into the habit of using the same phrases and petitions over and over again whenever we pray, possibly because we have not allowed the Holy Spirit to help us to think through the different subjects afresh, or to get any new insight into his wishes and plans? In that case, of course, these well-sounding phrases and Scripture quotations are really the vain repetitions and nice sounding words against which our Lord has particularly warned us (Matt. 6:7).

Real intercession depends upon thoughts and desires created in us, and liberated through us, by the Lord of Love himself. Is it not beautifully possible that he then, from the broadcasting station of our minds, transmits his lovely, merciful, forgiving, healing, strengthening and creative thoughts to the minds of others, by whom they are picked up as impulses to open to light and life and love?

For we must also remember that prayer essentially is the contact of our minds with the mind of God, resulting in a real conversation with him. But as he is God, and we are his beloved children, our prayer will take the form of a conversation in which we not only speak to him, but also listen to him and learn of him. Real meditation, as it is inspired in our minds and directed by the Holy Spirit, must surely be a most vital part of prayer, and even of intercession. Meditating on God's Word, and longing for others to understand it too, is part of the broadcasting to which we are called.

Another very important thing to remember, and which I for one have been all too prone to forget, is that all real desire in our hearts (wills) is prayer, because God looks on the thoughts of the heart and sees what our real desires are. It is the things which we really want, and not necessarily the things that our mouths are saying what we want, that is the real prayer which God perceives.

Therefore when we are in contact with him, all the desires of our hearts are really prayers, all our thoughts are creative. No wonder our Lord urged so solemnly that we should abide in him, have our minds stayed upon him. We really possess our mental faculties simply and solely that we may use them under the direction and control of the Holy Spirit. It is this which differentiates human beings from animals, namely this faculty of communicating with God through the contact of our minds with his.

When the prophets of old claimed over and over again that the Lord said, or that the word of the Lord came to them, they meant that God spoke to them in their thoughts, and clearly put his own thoughts into their minds. This is not an experience which comes to us passively, or when we abandon our minds to receive thoughts out of the blue, a most dangerous proceeding considering all the unnumbered minds around us broadcasting evil thought waves. No! It involves the most active thinking possible on our part, in cooperation with the Holy Spirit himself. And thus every unholy and unloving thought will instantly be recognized as a traitor thought seeking entrance from the realm of evil thinking.

This new understanding of the glory and heavenly privilege of prayer and intercession, which has recently come flooding into my mind like a sea of light, sweeping away the old idea of intercession as a dull and laborious duty, has also given me a completely new slant on the really awful importance laid upon us of separating from everything inconsistent with being a Christian. If we are going to be God's transmitters, our minds must be shut and garrisoned against every approach of evil thought waves. Therefore every avenue by which they might enter into our thought realm must be guarded.

It seems to me that many of us should face up in a completely new way to the possibility that we are allowing the enemy to transmit to our minds (through such things as the radio programs we carelessly listen to, through television broadcasts, through multitudes of magazines, periodicals, daily papers, and in a thousand other ways) thoughts and suggestions from minds that are utterly worldly, perhaps corrupted and distorted by lovelessness, hate and impurity.

God cannot transmit through minds which are busy receiving the wrong kind of thought waves. We are forbidden to judge, but we may warn one another, by sharing our experiences. And if we feel a little doubtful of someone else's ideas, we shall certainly do well to remember what the Apostle Paul wrote concerning the guarding of our thought realms.

"Now I am going to appeal to you personally, by the gentleness and sympathy of Christ himself . . . I am afraid that I shall have to do some plain speaking to those of you who will persist in reckoning that our activities are on the purely human level. The truth is that though of course we lead normal human lives, the battle we are fighting is on the spiritual level . . . for the destruction of the enemy's strongholds . . . We fight to capture every thought until it acknowledges the authority of Christ." And again in Romans 12:2, "Don't let the world around you squeeze you into its own mould, but let God remould your minds from within" (2 Cor. 10:1-5, *Letters to Young Churches* by J. B. Phillips).

Every thought should be holy, that is, separated from all that is antagonistic to holy love. All our thoughts are to be alive with the love of God. For if it is really true that all thought is either creative or destructive, and is going forth from our minds into the vast universe of the realm of thought, then our thoughts are more lasting and powerful in their effects than our words and deeds can ever be.

We are thinking spirits, and our spirits appear to be separated from each other by our material and temporal bodies. But it seems possible that our thoughts go out into the universe of thought, over distances beyond our conceiving, touching and influencing for good or ill every other thought wave which picks them up. No wonder we are in need of salvation, a deliverance and cleansing and transforming salvation, greater and more important than anything we have understood hitherto.

This fact about our thoughts may help to explain something which perhaps has often both terrified and perplexed us. We may have wondered from whence come those awful, unclean, dark thoughts which even earnest Christians are sometimes horrified to find surging into their minds with almost irresistible force? May they not have been broadcast by evilly disposed minds, which are pouring into the universe of thought their corrupt and hateful poisons? And because we have, of our own free will (through some wrong thought-attitude we chose to indulge in), allowed our minds to become out of harmony with our Savior, these thoughts have been able to enter and remain.

As sons and daughters of God we are called to be partakers of the divine nature, and when we are in Christ we have this power to transmit his thoughts and love to others. Salvation means to be gloriously delivered from the old nature—i.e. our corrupted thought life, and to experience the kingdom of God, the reign of love, established within us instead. Anything less must be a spurious salvation, and a child of God must never be content with anything short of the eternal life of God himself, in Jesus Christ, filling and transforming and controlling his whole being.

Of course we are children of God from the first moment that we believe in Jesus Christ and respond to him, long before the thought realm of our minds has been brought wholly under his control. His salvation and delivering power is a gloriously progressive thing. But, oh, how pitifully slowly some of us, myself not least, come to experience this full salvation, the life more abundant and fruitful, as our whole thought life is gradually brought under the control of the Holy Spirit!

How many of us have distorted the idea of salvation to mean simply pardon for our sins, and deliverance from hell hereafter. But our Lord taught that we can be in danger of hell fire here and now, by giving up our minds to wrong habits of thought (Matt. 5:22). For is not hell the awful condition of being a slave and captive to wrong thoughts and sinful, unloving desires; the condition of those who cut themselves off from contact with the saving love of God?

But is it really possible for us to experience such a salvation as we have been thinking about, here and now, while we are on earth? Can we really live day by day and moment by moment, with a mind completely garrisoned by the Holy Spirit, so that every thought is brought into captivity to Christ? Yes, we can. In the next chapters we shall consider two vital principles which our Lord himself taught and practiced, and which we must practice too if we wish to experience full salvation and deliverance and to become real intercessors or transmitters for God.

The two principles are these:

1. Faith which brings us into contact with our Savior Jesus Christ.
2. Love which brings us into contact with our fellow men.

CHAPTER 3
Faith

"Today if ye will hear his voice, harden not your hearts" (Heb. 3:15).

"Take heed lest there be in you an evil heart of unbelief, in departing from the living God" (Heb. 3:12).

"Lord, increase our faith" (Luke 17:5).

"If thou canst believe, all things are possible to him that believeth" (Mark 9:23).

Our Lord emphasized over and over again that faith is the one connecting link by which we make contact with God. Unbelief cuts us off from God, and faith unites us with him, making us receptive of his eternal life. "And this life is in his Son" (1 John 5:11).

Personally, I cannot help thinking that though the Bible talks about faith continually, and affirms that it is a vital necessity, very many of us in this present generation have very hazy, not to say distorted, ideas as to what faith is, and also what the Bible means by unbelief.

Generally speaking, do we not assume that faith in God and faith in Jesus Christ means believing that the things which the Bible tells us about God are true and that all the doctrines and teaching about Jesus Christ are to be accepted as true likewise. We have come to suppose that accepting as true all that the Bible says means that we have faith, and that if we believe that he died for our sins, and his death was indeed an atonement for the sins of the world, then we have saving faith, and have passed from death unto life.

This tendency on the part of some to give to the word "faith" the meaning of believing or accepting something as true has caused a great deal of tragic confusion and perplexity. For many of us have really believed all the statements in the gospels, and never doubted that it was true that our Lord died for the sins of the world, including our own. But nothing happened. It simply didn't work. We found ourselves still as completely cut off from the life and power of God in actual experience, as ever we were before we believed these "saving truths."

To believe something is true is mere mental belief, and although it is intensely important that we should believe things that are true, and disbelieve those that are not, we cannot correctly name the former attitude faith, and the latter unbelief, in the Bible sense of the words.

From painful personal experience, I feel that we cannot make this point too clear. Some earnest Christians are so sure that, if a man will really confess he believes Christ died for his sins, he is immediately saved, and can be assured that he has passed from death unto life. And then they are pained and filled with wonder when all too often nothing happens as a result.

But knowing something to be true is not the same as exercising faith. As James has pointed out, "the devils also believe, and tremble," but it doesn't have the least saving effect upon them (James 2:19). And is it not all too true that many a person who believes all the fundamental doctrines exercises, in actual fact, no faith at all, and, with considerable knowledge of truths in his head, quite obviously remains out of contact with the transforming life and power of Christ?

Real faith, as the Bible conceives of it, is responsiveness to God, who has made himself known to us in Jesus Christ. And unbelief is unresponsiveness, the hardening of our wills in a refusal to respond as we ought to that which we know is true.

Faith is the response of our wills to the will of God. It is willingness to see God's will and willingness to obey it.

A man, as we have already seen, may believe with his mind all the Christian doctrines, and yet continue to harden his will as an adamant stone, refusing to respond in obedience to what he knows God is telling him to do.

A man may have the queerest notions and errors in his head (probably learned from the particular church or Christian group in which he was brought up), and yet may long and hunger with all his heart, and will, to respond to God as he has revealed himself in Jesus Christ, and to obey him according to the light he has. And that willing responsiveness is faith.

It is the one primary condition for which our Lord looks, and when he finds it he finds that which delights him and enables him to have his way in that person's life. "All things are possible to him that believeth" (Mark 9:23). But when that willing responsiveness is lacking, he can "there do no mighty work because of unbelief" (Matt. 13:58, Mark 6:5). Unbelief is the hardening of the will in disobedience to light which has been seen and recognized.

In the Old Testament we have the history of the Children of Israel in the wilderness,

38

and it is a tragic history of unbelief. Yet we cannot help seeing clearly that their unbelief did not consist in doubting God's ability, or power, or even his willingness to help them. They really couldn't doubt his power, having seen the miracles of the plagues in Egypt, and having actually walked through the Red Sea dryfoot. For years they had been kept alive in a howling wilderness, fed with manna from heaven.

No, they did not doubt God's power, but they were absolutely unwilling to respond and cooperate with his will, because they did not like, or want, the things he chose for them, but wanted their own will to be done instead.

Their whole attitude all the time was this: "We know God can perform signs and wonders, but if he wants us to be his people and to follow him, he must continue to do them. He must always feed us with the kind of food we want, and give us water in abundance. And he must never allow us to suffer any real trial or loss, or test us uncomfortably in any way. If he agrees to this, then we will follow further; if not, we will turn back to Egypt. If he doesn't make life easier and give us what we want, then we shall do better to return to the situation we left. There is no point in following him, if he is going to lead us into danger and hardship and suffering and tribulation."

So from first to last the narrative of the wilderness journeyings is a history of mur-

murings and threats of returning back to the land of Egypt. They would follow God and be his people if he gave them what they wanted, but they were definitely not interested in what he wanted.

It was this attitude which Moses called "tempting God." Not testing him. God loves us to put him to the test and to prove that he does what he promises. We put him to the proof when we obey him and so experience his faithfulness. But we tempt him when we say, "We will follow and cooperate only if you give us what we want. Do what we ask you to do, or we will turn back and follow no further." How many a professing Christian is like those professing Israelites in this respect!

This is what an evil heart of unbelief consists in, a hardening of our will against God's will, simply because we do not like what he has chosen for us, but want our own will to be done, or the circumstances that we don't like to be altered, and demand that he should let us have what we want.

Again, we read that when our Lord was in Nazareth, "He could there do no mighty work . . . and he marvelled at their unbelief" (Mark 6:5, 6). Now we can be quite sure that the people of Nazareth believed that he could work miracles, and that he could heal their own sick folk and give sight to their blind. His power to do this had been so gloriously demonstrated in so many other places that they cannot have doubted it;

indeed Mark expressly states that they said, "What is this wisdom that is given to this man that even such mighty works are wrought by His hands?" (Mark 6:2). No, the reason why he could do no mighty work there was because they added, "Is not this the carpenter, the son of Mary . . . and they were offended at him" (v. 3).

The fact was that, though no doubt they would have liked to have their sick folk healed, they were unwilling that Jesus, the carpenter's son, should be the one to do it. Their wills were set against him being accepted as a prophet, and, still more, as the Messiah. They would make no response of faith, no matter how many gracious and blessed miracles he wrought, because they did not want to have to acknowledge One whom they despised.

If they did acknowledge him, they would have to follow him. And who was going to follow the son of Joseph the carpenter and to admit his mother and brothers and sisters, those common peasant people, to a place of preeminence. Not they! They preferred to remain as they were, thank you, and he could go elsewhere to heal sick folk. That was the essence of their unbelief.

But where our Lord Jesus found faith—that is, eagerness to come to him and to obey his teaching—there he gladly demonstrated that all things are possible to him that believeth; to those who prove they possess a true faith by willingness to respond to

God's will, cost what it may, and to express that faith in obedience.

Some Christians do not like such an interpretation of faith because it is too challenging, and they will exclaim: "Oh! that is exalting works. But I believe in salvation by faith alone. I bank my all on the atoning death of Christ, and I am not under law, but under grace." But all the time, perhaps, the will is hardened, refusing to face the light and to respond to the promptings of the Holy Spirit. It is much more comfortable and easy to assume that faith only means believing that certain true things are true, than to face the fact that it means responsive obedience, and that the Apostle James was absolutely right when he asserted that faith without works is dead, i.e. that a belief which does not express itself in some obedient response or action, is not true faith at all.

This is the faith that saves, a responsive will, utterly yielded to God, and ready to be obedient.

Does not this throw much light on our Lord's teaching about the prayer of faith? "Jesus said unto them, Have faith in God. For verily I say unto you, that whosoever shall say unto this mountain 'Be thou removed and be thou cast into the sea;' and shall not doubt in his heart, but shall believe that those things which he saith shall come to pass, he shall have whatsoever he saith" (Mark 11:22-23).

Many have been perplexed by this statement about the mountain, and have supposed that failure to remove a mountain would be proof of lack of faith. But when we understand that faith is responsiveness to God, we realize at once that our Lord simply said, "If you are really responsive to God's will, and he reveals to you that it is his will that an actual mountain should be removed, then, quite literally, you will be able to cast it into the sea. Nothing he wants you to do will be impossible. But this doesn't mean that anything you want to do, or may decide to attempt on your own initiative, will be possible. But every God-prompted and God-initiated project is possible. Nothing is impossible that God really tells you to do.

In that wonderful chapter on faith, Hebrews 11, how clearly the fact is illustrated that faith is responsiveness! It is one long list of men and women who were prompted by God to amazing actions and feats of all kinds, and who responded in obedience. That responsive obedience on their part, even when they were called to attempt what looked like utter impossibilities, or even mad follies, is called their faith. They were first of all sure of what God wanted them to do, and then the attitude of their will was, "Now we are going to obey and attempt it."

So we read of Abraham, called to go out, going out, though not knowing wither he went, and when he was tried, offering up his own son; of Noah, called to build an ark inland far away from the sea, building it, and so saving his family; of Moses giving up all the wealth and pleasure of Egypt when he was tried, in order to suffer affliction with the people of God. And so on, down through the glowing account of that great army of heroes of faith.

Ought we not to search ourselves and see whether we really have this true faith, or only an intellectual assent to the truths taught us in the Scriptures with no will to obey? Faith is essentially an attitude of heart, i.e. of the will, and it has little to do with feeling—not even feeling sure of God.

It is this faith, then, this responsiveness to the will of God, which is the one vital means of contact with God, and of living in union with him. And where faith makes this contact with God as he offers himself to us in Jesus Christ our Saviour, there his life pours into us, his power fills us, and his Holy Spirit controls the whole realm of our thought life.

But let that response cease, even for a moment, through a resistance to some point in the known will of God, and that vital contact is broken; the power can no longer reach us, nor can it flow through us, until contact is again made by faith, which is willingness to respond in obedience at the very point where we resisted before, and so broke the contact.

How necessary it is therefore that those

who wish to be God's transmitters abide in him continually. We do not pluck ourselves out of God's keeping and love when we resist, but we do most inevitably disconnect ourselves from his power when we knowingly resist his will in any way. A hardening of our hearts means a resistance of our wills, for the heart is the throne room, the innermost place of control. And in the heart, either self-will is on the throne, or the will of God.

And now again, to emphasize the great and all important truth that in the Scriptures it is the Lord Jesus Christ himself who is revealed as the point of contact with God. In him, and in him alone, is this life and power available to us. The incarnation was for this one great purpose, that we human beings might be united to God through Jesus Christ our Lord, who is the Son of God and Son of Man, the meeting place where eternal life can break through to human beings. This life is in his Son.

And it is therefore faith in Jesus Christ, response to him and obedience to his teaching which, as it were, plugs us into the source of life and power. Indeed there is no other point in all the universe where this contact with eternal life can be made. It is the Son of God, who is also become Son of Man, who told us this great and glorious truth when he said, "He that believeth on me (i.e. responds to me) hath eternal life . . .

45

I am come that ye might have life, and that ye might have it more abundantly. I lay down my life for the sheep."

The loveliest and most glorious place in all the universe is the point where we contact him, our Lord and Savior, and accept his teaching as the standard by which we are to live.

If there should be someone reading this who realizes with a pang of pain and sorrow that this most wonderful of contacts has not yet been made, there is another lovely word to be added. Faith is one of God's gifts. We do not have to labor to try and produce it ourselves. To every poor slave of self who really desires it, is given the power to respond in obedience to our Lord and Savior Jesus Christ.

The great struggle to yield a stubbornly resisting will is not something which we can bring to an end in our own strength. But if God's gracious, creative love thoughts have found an entrance into our minds, and awakened in us a longing to respond to him, and to be liberated from the horrible slavery of self, and exposure to all the evil and poisonous and dark thoughts which torment the minds of men, then, if we ask, the power to respond will be given, and the yielding will become possible.

The meeting place of his will and our will is at the cross. For it was there, on the cross, that he laid down his will and his life for us, and it is there that we, too, are enabled to lay down our will and yield our life to him, and, in that yielding, the contact is made which unites us to him forever.

CHAPTER 4
Love

"A new commandment I give unto you, that ye love one another: as I have loved you, that ye also love one another. By this shall all men know that ye are my disciples, if ye have love one to another" (John 13:34, 35— Our Lord Jesus Christ).

"If ye fulfil the royal law according to the Scripture, 'Thou shalt love thy neighbor as thyself,' ye shall do well" (James 2:8— James, the Lord's brother).

"Beloved, let us love one another, for love

is of God, and everyone that loveth is born of God and knoweth God. He that loveth not, knoweth not God, for God is love" (1 John 4:7, 8). "My little children, let us not love in word, neither in tongue, but in deed and in truth" (1 John 3:18—The First Epistle of John).

"See that ye love one another with a pure heart, fervently" (1 Pet. 1:22—The Apostle Peter).

". . . Love one another: for he that loveth another hath fulfilled the Law . . . Love worketh no ill to his neighbour, therefore love is the fulfilling of the law" (Rom. 13:8, 10—The Apostle Paul).

There were two things which our Lord emphasized all through his teaching: first, the supreme importance of faith as the only way to make contact with God; secondly, love as the one vital principle by which we maintain contact with our fellow men.

All the practical teaching our Lord gave in connection with the lives we are to live here on earth was summed up in the commandment to love. If we break the contact of love, by permitting ourselves to think thoughts of resentment, hate, bitterness, self-pity, jealousy, wrath, selfishness, or any other dark thoughts, then, no matter how nice or holy our audible petitions may sound, no matter how beautiful and lovely the collects we repeat, we have broken the contact, and have ceased to be God's transmitters.

Without love we can no more transmit God's life and thoughts and power and love to others, than our radio sets can transmit when the current is turned off. How the Apostle Paul knew this in his own experience! "If I have not love I am become as sounding brass, or a tinkling cymbal." "If I have not love, I am nothing." "If I have not love it profiteth me nothing" (1 Cor. 13:1-3).

We do need to remind ourselves of the challenging fact, that as long as we are thinking wrong, unloving thoughts about another person, we are antagonizing their thoughts against us, so that they simply will not tune in to our thought waves, or be receptive in any way. Therefore, so long as we maintain a wrong thought habit towards others, our prayers will be quite unavailing as far as those people are concerned, and it is nothing but hypocrisy to utter them.

But we must be careful not to be confused just here, as the enemy would like us to be. It is not a question of feelings. We may be swept by feelings which we cannot always control at once, of bitterness and anger and exasperation, etc. But if we really want, at the same time, to forgive and to feel loving towards those persons, then we may be sure we have not become disconnected, and the feelings will be cast out by the power of the Holy Spirit of Love in us.

The desire to love, and to forgive, and to get rid of the wrong feelings, shows that the contact still holds. It is wrong feelings welcomed and harbored and brooded upon that break the contact, not feelings which we cannot control, and from which we yearn passionately to be freed.

We can see therefore how necessary it is for every one who longs to transmit for God, to be able to detect and recognize instantly every poisonous thought which comes from the wrong source, and which is antagonistic to love, and which therefore will break off the contact we must maintain if we are to transmit to others the creative, redemptive love of God. This is indeed so vitally important, that our Lord carefully listed these thought poisons, and this list we shall be studying presently.

But the challenging truth is, that if we think these poisonous thoughts which he so particularly warns against, especially if we allow them to become habitual thought habits in our minds, then we not only break our contact with holy love and cease to transmit for God, but we are actually allowing the powers of evil to transmit their destructive, poisonous and injurious thoughts through us.

Is this really possible in a child of God? Yes, it is, but oh, how seldom we are warned against it!

Of course this does not mean that we lose our standing in Christ Jesus or cease to belong to him. He has assured us that when we commit ourselves to him, nothing can pluck us out of his hand. He has made himself responsible for us, weak and sinful as we are, and pledged himself to deliver us out of the powers of darkness into the Kingdom of Light. Nothing will be allowed to prevent that. But it does mean that when we allow the contact to be broken in our thought life, we actually permit the Enemy to use a transmitting station which belongs to God. And, judging by my own experience, we often allow this to happen just because we do not realize the awful possibility, and have comforted ourselves by saying that if we do not express our thoughts in words and deeds, they go no further and hurt no one. We need to face the truth and to be challenged by it.

What is the carnal Christianity which Paul so often warns his converts about? Surely it is just this: an up-and-down experience in which our thoughts are sometimes controlled by the Holy Spirit, and sometimes by spiritual wickedness in high places. If we understand this, we shall be warned, and "fore-warned is fore-armed." It is the exact experience which Paul so graphically described in Romans 7 (I quote from *Letters to Young Churches,* by J. B. Phillips).

"I am carnal, . . . and in practice what happens? My own behavior baffles me. For I find myself not doing (and thinking) what I really want to, but what I really loathe. In my own nature (which is the thought life) I am bound fast to the law of sin and death. It is an agonizing situation, and who on earth can set me free from the clutches of my own sinful nature (thought life)? I thank God there is a way out through Jesus Christ our Lord" (Rom. 7:14, 15, 23-25). The words in brackets are my own.

I think, though all may not agree, that we may rightly interpret the word *nature* as meaning our habitual thought habits and desires, because it is so utterly true that it is our thought habits which make us what we are and determine our character. The things we naturally think determine what sort of people we really are at rock bottom. And when we say we are sinful by nature, we really mean we are sinful in our thought life, and it is this which corrupts our visible life and conduct. For all visible living and conduct is the expression of the nature of the thoughts we think.

Good and evil are in conflict for the control of our thoughts and the use of our minds, and there is this strife going on within us all the time until we come under the complete control of the Holy Spirit, who then brings every thought into captivity to Christ. Then the up-and-down experience ceases, and the transmitting station is under the control of the One we longed to serve, Love himself. This is the full salvation which is promised us, and it is for eternity. Eternal life is to live thinking and expressing the creative thoughts and nature of God.

This is why no real Christian must dare to

tamper with the idea that full surrender is not essential, or that it doesn't much matter if we continue to be carnal Christians, living this low-level experience of habitual failure in the thought life.

We can never say, "Now I believe in the atoning death of Jesus Christ, and have received the forgiveness of sins, and so I am quite safe and need not aim at being a saint;" for the Bible teaches us that salvation means nothing less than the Kingdom of God made actual within us, the complete annexation by the Holy Spirit of our whole being. And if our thought life (where the seeds of sin originate) is not brought more and more fully under his control, we really are not experiencing salvation. There is no such thing as incomplete salvation, or imperfect Christian experience, sanctioned in the Bible.

Good William Law, writing about 1740, expressed this much more pithily than we are wont to hear it in our generation:

". . . God may be merciful to a low estate of piety, by reason of some pitiable circumstances that may attend it. But as soon as thou choosest such an estate of piety, it loses those pitiable circumstances, and instead of a low state of piety, is changed into a high state of impiety!"

Now let us consider briefly the thought attitudes destructive of love, which poison our own thought life, and which cut us off from the power of the Holy Spirit who longs to think in us, and which also make vital contact with our fellow men impossible. In short, the thought habits which make it impossible for God to use us as intercessors or transmitters of his saving power to others.

Our Lord outlines this list very carefully in the Sermon on the Mount; I shall only refer briefly, to each attitude, but we need to ponder over them again and again, and seek for fuller light upon the meaning of all he said.

This list is more fully cataloged for us in Matthew's Gospel, chapters 5, 6 and 7. There the Lord describes nine thought poisons of the most dangerous kind, and also gives the antidote for each one. But he begins that wonderful lesson on the realm of thought by stating nine healing and blessed attitudes of thought which maintain us in gloriously healthy and powerful contact with himself, and which guard the whole thought realm against invasion by enemy thoughts.

We have named this list the Beatitudes. The word *blessed* can be translated into modern speech as "healthy and happy;" and this reminds us that the Greek word for salvation is a word meaning perfect wholeness for spirit, soul and body.

1. Blessed—or healthy and happy—are: "The poor in spirit" (literally the beggars who have nothing of their own)—those

who live in the attitude of child-like and beggar-like dependence upon God for everything, joyfully receiving all that his bounty provides. They have no confidence in themselves, for they are bankrupts. Those who are habitually Christ-conscious instead of self-conscious.

2. "Blessed are they that mourn," or bewail themselves in penitence and sorrow for all sin in thought, and transgression in deed, or are distressed because of the malady and misery of the world: "They shall be comforted," by forgiveness and by experiencing union with the Lord.

3. "Blessed are the meek." Meekness is the opposite of self-assertion. It is an attitude of mind which accepts with joy the will of God, and bears and forgives all that is done against it, without resentment.

4. "Blessed are they that hunger and thirst for righteousness" with a passionate and continuous longing for rightness in thought, word and deed, and a corresponding hatred of wrongness. The attitude of mind which longs to keep open to the Light and to receive more light and life and love.

5. "Blessed are the merciful," the tender and compassionate in judgment, who will not criticize, but discern with the eye of love where help, and perhaps warning, is needed.

6. "Blessed are the pure in heart." Those with an honest and sincere desire to know the will of God, and to do it and who never rationalize their true motives.

7. "Blessed are the peacemakers." Those who delight in ending strife and discord and have a horror of sowing seeds of suspicion and dislike.

8. "Blessed are they that are persecuted for righteousness' sake." Those who willingly suffer for the Lord without self-pity or parade or bitterness.

9. "Blessed are ye, when men revile you and persecute you, and say all manner of evil against you falsely, for my sake." Those who accept with joy and praise and with no hint of murmuring or complaint, all that God sees fit to allow men to do and speak against them, accepting it as a glorious opportunity for practicing creative and forgiving thoughts about others.

These are only the briefest suggestions about verses which grow and shine with the glory of the Kingdom of Heaven. They are the thought attitudes of the inhabitants of Heaven and while we live on this earth, forming (if we are true Christians), "a colony of Heaven" (Phil. 3:20—Moffatt), we are told to enjoy the health and happiness of practicing them too. Thus the atmosphere and climate of Heaven will pervade the whole thought life of the children of God.

Now the opposites of these thought attitudes are the poisonous thoughts, and who amongst us has not known the darkness and unhappiness, yes, and perhaps the real physical diseases, which result from indulging habitually in such poisonous thoughts? For undoubtedly these thought habits, against which our Lord was so careful to warn us, are the cause of a great deal of the sickness and disease suffered in the bodies of many Christians. Here is the list of poisons, a list which we need to study and pray over individually with great care and attention.

1. All wrathful and disparaging thoughts about others, Matt. 5:21-26. Angry and disparaging and contemptuous thoughts are poisonous. They come from the realm of darkness. The word *raca* really means worthless fellow and "Thou fool" means impious one; or rebel. Even to disparage one another, our Lord said, is dangerous, for to despise any of our fellow men, and to think them not worth loving, is the attitude of those who choose hellish attitudes.

There is, however, a great difference between righteous wrath against wicked and cruel acts, and indulging in wrathful thoughts against those who do them.

A wicked act is an abomination to love, but an evildoer calls for compassion and a determination if possible to deliver him from his bondage to wickedness and from condemning himself to the state in which love is dead, the desire for good is gone, and escape from the slavery of one's loveless self is impossible.

2. *Impure and Lustful Thoughts, Ch. 5:27-32.* We have no possibility of estimating the number and force of such thoughts broadcast by enemy-controlled mind-stations in our generation, but judging by the frequent temptations to impurity of thought experienced by multitudes of horrified Christians, even by those who avoid the wrong sort of cinema shows, television programs and modern picture-periodicals, etc., the broadcasting of such thoughts must be on a most overwhelming scale.

As indeed it must have been in our Lord's day too, where it was so common a thing to find people possessed by unclean spirits. It is likely that many of the unutterably revolting crimes described on the front pages of our newspapers are the outcome of just such possession of the mind by unclean thoughts broadcast by others: it may even be, by other unclean thinkers, no longer in the flesh.

We do well to remember our Lord's warning against unclean, gangrenous thoughts. He challenges us to cut out of our lives anything and everything which causes us to stumble. Nothing is too drastic, he said, if it will keep these invading impurities out of our thought realm. The Holy Spirit will show us, each one individually, just what the cutting off must consist of in our own lives.

3. All Untrue, Unjust and Deceitful Thoughts are also Poisons, Ch. 5:33-37. To harbor any untrue and treacherous thoughts about others, even to indulge in gossip, is also deadly in its effect. To find a hateful kind of pleasure in such thoughts, and to entertain them willingly, is fatal. But these verses must also refer to dishonest thoughts and intentions, every secret thought or desire to make another person believe something which is not true.

4. All Thoughts of Retaliation and Revenge, Chapter 5:38-42. To brood on thoughts of revenge and spite is a deadly poisonous thought attitude and so is a spirit of grudging submission.

5. All Thoughts of Hate and Unwillingness to Forgive, Chapter 5:43-48. Even thoughts of hate and revenge against those who have proved themselves enemies are poisonous. Our Lord laid greater emphasis on the absolute necessity of willingness to forgive than on anything else. It might be a most astounding revelation to discover just how much disease, both bodily and mental is the direct outcome of a refusal to forgive, and the brooding on resentful, revengeful, bitter thoughts in our hearts.

As hate is the utter antithesis of love (which we know is the most creative and healing force in the universe), so hate must necessarily be the most destructive and death-producing force possible. The only cure, the only possible way to return to health, both of mind and body, is by opening at once to love, and begin loving the one we hated, forgiving him or her completely and determining never again to brood over the wrong done to us. Only so can we escape from the slow spiritual death which hate and refusal to forgive will bring to our whole personality.

6. *All Vainglorious and Self-Admiring Thoughts, Chapter 6:1-18*. Self-righteousness and self-display, with love of the limelight, seem deeply ingrained in the thinking habits of many real Christian people. The habit of comparing ourselves favorably with others and disparaging them in our thoughts is a secret sin about which many of us know a great deal. But like all thought sins, it is not really secret at all, but manifests itself quite unmistakably in the ways in which we draw attention to ourselves in public, perhaps in the habit of "modestly" sharing with others all the little victories and opportunities for Christian witness which we have found or made during the course of each day!

Under this heading must come, too, the secret habit of daydreaming vaingloriously about ourselves, indulging in many a private cinema show in our own imaginations, picturing ourselves as greatly used and much admired Christian workers. This is offering incense to self, and for some of us is the hardest of all inner thought snares and bondage to escape from. It not only has a deadly effect upon our minds, but it also makes us irritable, critical, and often almost impossible to get along with.

7. *Covetous and Ambitious Thoughts, Chapter 6:19-24.* Love of money and lust of riches, and a thought life largely controlled by this idolatry, was something our Lord warned against very seriously indeed, both in the Sermon on the Mount and on many other occasions. He stated emphatically, not that we are unlikely to love God if we love mammon, but that we cannot love and serve both God and mammon at the same time. It is literally impossible. It is strange how easily even good church members can forget this. Inordinate love of profits and possessions is not confined to worldly businessmen. It can play a very subtle part in ensnaring even a Christian's thought life.

8. *All Anxious and Worried Thoughts, Chapter 6:25-34.* Yes, our Lord did actually and most emphatically warn us against the thought habit of worry. We are not meant to picture a lot of imaginary troubles or difficulties in the future, or to dread disasters and illnesses, or to fret continuously lest we

lose our money, or job or health, and what shall we do then! Some people feel that it is an absolute impossibility to stop worrying about the future. Imaginative natures suffer most, but we may thankfully remind ourselves that, though the imagination is one of the greatest of all gifts which God has given us, it was never intended to be used in this way.

One of the loveliest uses for which the imagination is intended, however, is to enable us to put ourselves in the place of other people, thereby being better able to see how to help them. It is also meant to help us to make the most sensible and right plans for the future which it is possible to do, but never to worry.

Doctors and psychologists tell us so often and so plainly about the direful effect of worry on both bodies and minds, that we do not need to be told again about it. What we do need and long for, however, is to be told how we may escape from the agonizing bondage of worry and anxiety. And this (our Lord Jesus tells us in these verses), is possible by simple faith in a loving heavenly Father who delights in providing for his children.

If we suppose that faith only means believing that God is both able and willing to provide for us, we are not likely to get free of our worry. But as we have already seen, real faith is obedient response to God's will. The anxious person who expresses his mental belief in God's willingness to provide for him, even his delight in doing so, by acting in some way which really commits him to dependence upon God, will find his worries melt away like morning mist. But once again, the act of faith must be prompted by God, and not be selected by the worrier himself!

9. *All Judging and Critical Thoughts About Other People, Chapter 7:15.* Our Lord left this poisonous attitude to the last, perhaps so that he could emphasize it in a special way. For if there is one sin in the thought life more common than another, it is this brooding in our thoughts on the shortcomings, blemishes, failures and mistakes of others, until they give rise to inordinate exasperation in our minds and crush the thoughts of love in a truly awful way. This snare is so subtle that we often disguise from ourselves what we are really doing. We tell ourselves that we are holding these things in our minds so that we can pray for the aggravating persons, and so, even under the guise of prayer, we tear them to pieces and expose all their weak places.

Since it is so possible that thought really is able to travel and contact others, we are actually making it more difficult for people to get free from their blemishes, perhaps even binding them more tightly upon them. What we loose out of our minds, said the Lord, will disappear, but what we bind, remains. How many of our prayers are destructive, because they emphasize the faults of other people, instead of being creative in transmitting thoughts of God's lovely and gracious plans for deliverance and transformation?

These are only brief suggestions to call attention to the teaching of our Lord on this subject. If we understand which thought habits are poisonous, we shall long to yield ourselves completely to the reign of the Holy Spirit of Love, and will never rest until he has transformed us by the renewing of our minds. Then the very first whiff, as it were, of one of these poisonous thought suggestions will cause us to cast them from us with as much horror and loathing as we would reject a cup of poison as soon as we suspected what was in it. Then, too, we shall be prepared to do what the Lord so vehemently urged, to cut out of our lives completely everything which we find encourages and stimulates in us the indulgence of thinking wrong thoughts.

Lastly, there is our Lord's teaching in the Sermon on the Mount about prayer. Here he gives us what the Christian Church considers to be the model prayer (Matt. 6:9-13). The Lord's Prayer seems to sum up the desires which characterize a heart or will that abides plugged into the life of the God of love. For these seven statements and petitions are really seven heart's desires, the seven perfect desires which together make perfect love. The Lord's Prayer is not so much intended for repetition as for presenting a standard of desire to which we are to conform.

THE SEVEN HEART'S DESIRES OF PERFECT LOVE

"Our Father which art in heaven." The desire to be kept continually in the attitude of child-like love and trust and delight in the Father's presence. To be utterly dependent on him, and utterly like him. To live in heaven even while here on earth, for heaven is the realm where everyone thinks and expresses the creative love-thoughts of the heavenly Father.

"Hallowed be thy name." The desire to share in the nature of Holy Love himself. To be completely separated (which is the meaning of hallowed) from every thought which is not in harmony with holy love. Passionate thankfulness for the glorious truth, that the name and nature of God is love.

"Thy Kingdom come; thy will be done on earth as it is done in heaven." The desire that the kingdom of God should be established in every human heart, so that Love shall reign on earth even as he does in heaven. A consuming desire to cooperate in every way possible in bringing this to pass.

"Give us this day our daily bread." This surely is a hunger and desire of mind as well as of body, a longing for communion with God himself, that we may be fed by him in soul as well as in body. The desire to receive from him that which will strengthen us, and cause us to grow spiritually. "For man doth not live by bread alone, but by every word which proceedeth out of the mouth of God" (Matt. 4:3).

"And forgive us our debts as we forgive our debtors." The longing desire of the heart both to be forgiven, and to be able to forgive, and thus be made like our Redeemer; able to transmit God's life to others.

"And lead us not into temptation, but deliver us from evil." A desire to be kept recoiling from every thought of evil, a yearning to be kept holy; separated from all that is unlike God. A longing to be strengthened to cut off all that we know has the power to tempt us and incline us to thoughts which are contrary to holy love.

"For thine is the kingdom, the power and the glory, for ever and ever, Amen." The desire to be kept in an attitude of heart and mind which adores and magnifies and praises the God of love continually, which goes through each day praising God for everything. The desire to be kept from entertaining a single murmuring or complaining or self-pitying

thought, and that Love himself shall be the center and object of all praise, for ever and for ever.

May these seven desires, which sum up the perfect desires of our Lord's own heart, and his own attitude and habits of thought, be realized in us also. For as long as this is the attitude of our hearts, we may be joyfully sure that we are abiding in him, and so are able to receive and transmit God's thoughts of creative love, without any effort or struggle or strain on our part.

Undoubtedly God, who so loves variety (as he has revealed in his creative activities) and who appears to be so uninterested in uniformity, will use his children's thought lives in very different ways. Probably he has different thought ministries for each of us. Some may be called to wrestle in prayer, and some to make spiritual discoveries and think his thoughts after him in a great variety of ways. But if we are abiding in our Lord and Savior, the lovely truth is evident that all our thoughts of love and goodwill and longing to help others, of pity and understanding sympathy and compassion, are a form of intercession, for these thoughts are broadcast and transmitted to those whom God yearns to help and save and bless.

We pray without ceasing when all our thoughts are under the control of the Holy Spirit, whether we think them when we are on our knees in our own rooms, or at the communion table, or in the kitchen, or office, or business store, in the bus or train or on the street. For intercession is not primarily our hearts pleading with God, but God transmitting his power through us.

Oh! that he may indeed raise up an ever-growing army of intercessors around the world, who will be the transmitters of his saving light and life and love; until he comes again to establish his reign over the whole earth!

Will you enlist in this army?

CHAPTER 5
Answers to Some Queries

After this little booklet was printed, I received a number of very kind and interesting letters, in some of which questions were asked. And when a second edition was prepared, it seemed a good opportunity to consider some of these questions and to include the answers in this booklet.

The first and by far the most important query was phrased in some such words as these:

1. There does not seem to be very much Scripture, if any, to support your suggestion that our minds are broadcasting stations from which our thoughts go forth, and that intercession largely consists in being used to transmit God's thoughts to others.

If the Bible does not definitely tell us that our minds are transmitting stations from which our thoughts are going forth all the time, yet it lays the most terrific emphasis upon our thoughts, warning us against the ones which we now know are so poisonous to our bodily health, and challenging us to allow the Holy Spirit to have them completely under his control.

In this connection it is also intensely interesting to ponder on such passages in the Gospels of Matthew 15:19 and Mark 7:21, where it says "out of the heart proceed evil thoughts . . . ," etc., as well as a number of passages in Luke (5:22, 6:8, 11:17, 9:47), where it states that Jesus knew or perceived their thoughts.

The Bible of course repeatedly tells us that God knows the thoughts of our hearts, and probably the picture we have in our minds is of a great omniscient thought reader, whose x-ray eyes can pierce into the innermost recesses of our brains. But it can just as well be true that he knows all our thoughts, because we are so made that they are proceeding forth out of us all the time in thought waves as definite and real as sound and light waves.

My sole purpose in so emphasizing this possibility is, that if there is the merest likelihood that this is actually the case, we have a tremendous incentive to allow the Holy Spirit to control our thoughts, and to use them as he pleases. For me, personally, it clears up some of the most perplexing problems connected with our Lord's teaching about prayer.

There are many things, which we now know to be facts, about which the Bible is completely silent. For instance, if it tells us nothing about thought waves, neither does it give us any hint that there are sound and light waves. And yet we know that the latter have always been scientific facts, even though earlier generations knew nothing about them. Now that we do know about them and how to use them, our way of life has been completely revolutionized.

Again, the Bible does not specifically tell us that certain thought habits, such, for instance, as "bitterness, wrath, anger . . . malice," etc. (Eph. 4:31), can radically affect our bodies, and if persisted in can produce in us the exact symptoms and diseases which appear in our bodies through the introduction of microbes, germs and other infections from without. But doctors now tell us that this is a proved fact and that unhealthy mental attitudes of thought are likely to produce in us definite physical reactions.

For example, fear attacks the digestive system, worry can cause over-acidity in the stomach, anger upsets the intestines, as probably any persons subject to violent rages have easily discovered for themselves. But though the Bible does not give us this information, it does again and again most solemnly warn us against these very emotions and attitudes of mind which we now know to be so destructive in their effects upon our bodies as well as our personalities. It does not explain just how they work us harm but it exhorts us over and over again to lay them aside altogether.

2. Your interpretation of the parable of the importunate widow in Luke 18 seems quite different to its obvious meaning and the usual interpretation given.

I must admit that to me the most obvious thing about this parable is that the usual interpretation raises the most extraordinarily perplexing question! i.e. Why does the Lord in this parable so urge the importance, indeed the necessity, for importunity, when it seems to contradict everything else which he taught about prayer in other places? For importunity is as unlike the attitude of child-like trust in a heavenly Father who knows all our needs before we ask him (Matt. 6:32) as it is possible to be.

If the obvious meaning of the parable is that we are to go on and on asking God for the same things, even though he keeps us waiting a long time for the answer, or even seems to refuse our request, but will give in to us in the end if we persist in asking long enough, then it does raise a tremendous question in our minds: why?

For we would never urge our own children to keep coming to us over and over again, in order to remind us of what they want! Nor would we exhort them to believe that if they importune us, in other words badger us long enough, we will give them what they desire; but if they cease their importuning too soon, we will not give it to them. That is the very last idea that we would want them to get into their minds.

Then why must the heavenly Father be importuned in this way? The answer often given is that he wants to test us and to strengthen our faith. But why should continual asking be considered faith, when in the natural realm we know instinctively that we express our faith in a friend whose help we have asked, not by continually reminding him of his promise to do so, but by waiting quietly and confidently for him to act in the way he promised? And we feel that it would be a definite sign of unbelief in his willingness to help us, or perhaps a doubt whether he is sufficiently interested in us to remember his promise, if we keep telephoning him every day, or writing to remind him of our need.

No, if the meaning of the parable is that God wants us to keep on importuning himself, then it is very perplexing indeed. But if it is true that he has so devised things that he needs our continual prayer for others, as a means by which he himself can continually importune those people, then our bewilderment dies away, and we can see at once that our prayers can become a great weapon which we and he can wield together.

Then the message of the parable would seem to be, if the unjust and unresponsive judge was at last willing to be overcome by a weak widow woman who kept importuning him in her own strength, how much more true it is that if we allow God to importune others through us, that he will prevail in the end, though it may need long patience, and a continued barrage of his importunity transmitted through us his intercessors.

Of course I do not mean to suggest that this is the only purpose of our prayers, nor the only way by which God answers prayer. For as we know so clearly, both from the Scriptures and in our own experience, he has innumerable ways by which he brings his will to pass.

He has infinite power and boundless other resources at his disposal.

We know, too, that the throne of grace is surrounded by his angels and his ministering spirits, all ready to obey his commands and to be sent forth on behalf of his people. But it does seem possible that as far as reaching the thoughts and wills of human beings is concerned, this power that we all have of transmitting thoughts to others may be his specially chosen and most effective means of reaching them and this is why the Scriptures so urgently suggest that he does need our cooperation, because it is the method which he himself has devised.

I should like once again to make it quite clear that not for one moment do I suggest that we should try to pray by transmitting our own thoughts to others. The clear teaching of the Bible is that we are to turn our thoughts to God himself, and make known our petitions unto him. This is the way in which the Lord's people have interceded down through the ages, under the control of the Holy Spirit, without understanding how it worked, or just how God used their prayers; and it is the way for us too.

At the end of this parable there is another verse which often perplexed me also: verses 6 and 7. "Hear what the unjust judge saith. And shall not God avenge his own elect which cry day and night unto him, though he bear long with them? Yea, he shall avenge them speedily."

Why should God choose to tarry and have long patience before avenging his elect and executing vengeance on those who afflict his people? Why not condemn and punish evil doers at once, and avenge the innocent speedily?

Here again it seems to me that this interpretation of intercession, as allowing God to plead with others through us, gives a very satisfactory answer. For through the very

ones who are being oppressed, he is able
and willing to importune the evil doers over
and over again, to see if they can be per-
suaded to turn from their wicked ways and
to be saved, rather than have to suffer judgment and destruction.

This is completely in harmony with the
Lord's teaching in Matt. 5:44: "I say unto
you, love your enemies, bless them that
curse you, do good to them that hate you,
and pray for them which despitefully use
you and persecute you." This is why the
Lord has long patience with evil doers, if by
any means (and most of all through intercession) he can save them.

But if the evil doers prove adamant, then
at last vengeance must be executed on them.
And this brings me to the third query.

3. Why could not Abraham himself have been the
intercessor for the cities of the plain, and have
saved them?

Of course this same question could also be
asked in connection with Ezekiel and Jere-
miah, both of whom tell us that God looked
for an intercessor in their day and found
none (see chapter 2).

The Bible does teach that it is possible for
men to prove so adamant, and to persist in
evil for so long, and to become so completely corrupted by it, that God judges that definite, drastic action must at last be taken, just
as a doctor comes to the conclusion that the
time has come to amputate a limb which has

turned gangrenous. That perhaps is why Abraham did not feel at liberty to go on pleading for the cities if there were less than ten righteous persons in them. For there comes a time when judgment of some sort must intervene and oppressors must be made to cease from wronging their innocent victims.

The Scriptures which speak about the end of the age definitely seem to indicate that this will be the case, and that there will be some whom it proves impossible to influence through the preaching of the gospel, or through intercession. Then the last terrible judgments must take place. But that time will not come until all who can be influenced have had their chance.

Such crises have occurred many times in history. In Ezekiel 14:14 we hear the words of the Lord about one such terrible occasion. Four times over the word of the Lord came to Ezekiel saying, "Though these three men, Noah, Daniel and Job, were in the land, they should deliver but their own souls by their righteousness, saith the Lord." And yet these three men were perhaps the three greatest intercessors of all time.

But there is this comforting thought for those of us who intercede for loved ones. If in any individual case those we intercede for prove adamant, and God deals with them by allowing some kind of judgment to overtake them, our intercession of course need not cease but rather should be strengthened. But it will then take the form of passionate desire that the judgment (which is always in mercy) may be able to effect what gracious importunity alone, apparently, could not do, and may bring them at last to repentance and faith. In this connection I love that beautiful passage in Rev. 8:1-6. There John tells us that just as the last terrible trumpets of judgment were about to sound, he was shown what was taking place in heaven at the same time.

"Another angel came and stood at the altar, having a golden censor, and there was given unto him much incense, that he should offer it with the prayers of all saints upon the golden altar which was before the throne. And the smoke of the incense with the prayers of the saints ascended up before God, out the angel's hand." Yes, there were the Redeemed with their Lord, still interceding while the unrepentant on earth were about to suffer terrible judgments, praying, surely, that judgment might accomplish the mighty purposes of God in bringing hardened sinners to repentance.

4. And now for the last query, which has been repeated more than once.

In your next edition, do you think you could explain a little more clearly how to practice intercession, and some method by which we can get rid of celestial shopping lists without a guilty conscience?

I must confess that I am most unwilling to make the attempt! We are all so different, and one particular method cannot help everybody. It would be terrible to stumble anyone by giving the idea that they should change their habit of intercession and try to adapt it to another's; so the first thing to be said is this: if your habit of prayer satisfies you, and brings the results you long for, most certainly stick to it—lists and all! Especially if you have been practicing that method happily and successfully for years. For it is most unlikely that your Lord will have allowed you to go on praying year after year in a way which does not satisfy him, without putting a longing desire in your heart to find some better way.

Secondly, if the suggestion in this book about the use which God may make of our prayers seems to you a difficult and perplexing interpretation, then of course don't bother with it. It is the actual going to the throne of grace and the personal heart-to-heart talks with the God of all grace, which is the real prayer and intercession, and we can practice that without understanding just how God may choose to use our prayers.

If on the other hand you are one of those who are definitely dissatisfied with your prayer life, and are finding intercession both laborious and lifeless, and all too often without results, why not try laying aside the lists for a while and just converse naturally and as simply as a child, with the Lord. Speak to him about your friends and loved ones, and all whom he brings to your remembrance, and any particular needs of theirs which you know about. I myself have given up trying to discuss the faults and failures of others with the Lord, and now pray for things that will make those I pray for happier and lovelier and more fruitful for him.

If there are on your prayer list the names of people that you really know very little about, then ask the Lord to use you for a moment or two to send thoughts of his love to them, or of joy or peace or comfort.

Try and picture each one for whom you pray, and ask to be helped to understand if they have any special need, and if there is anything he would have you do to help them, or anything in your own thought attitude towards them that needs to be corrected. If nothing comes to your mind, just pass on quietly to the next name on the list.

For we must realize that in this matter the Holy Spirit is much more anxious to help us even than we are to be helped. He knows the needs of each one, and he will bring to your remembrance those who need your help at some particular moment, or who, through circumstances you know nothing about, are now open to receive God's thoughts and love.

I think, too, we can get much help

through reading the accounts given in the Bible of the great intercessors, such as Abraham, Moses, Samuel, Daniel, David, and a host of others. Notice that their intercessions took the form of a personal conversation with God himself. So often our own intercessions are a long monologue, as I have before suggested, and nothing is more unreal than a monologue in the realm of prayer. Too easily it becomes simply a list of pious suggestions, instead of burning desires, and if the list is a very long one, is all too likely to degenerate into a repetition over and over again of "And please bless so and so," with only the names altered.

Then, too, there are the litanies and collects and written prayers which help so many of the Lord's children, but which seem so strange to those who are not accustomed to them. They are the recorded prayers and heart's desires of other Christians in other generations. If they create in our hearts a similar desire each time that we repeat them; a desire corresponding to the words, then they do indeed become a powerful means of help in intercession.

For if it is true that God uses our thought waves, then something approximating to these God-inspired desires may be awakened in the minds and hearts of those we are praying for, just as has been the case over and over again down through the centuries, ever since those same desires were first awakened in the hearts of the Lord's servants who recorded them that they might be a help to us too.

If, on the other hand, the collects, or written prayers, which we use do not create in our hearts a corresponding desire, then on those occasions they are, of course, merely formal and empty phrases.

Above all, don't be afraid to experiment until you find the way in which it is right for you to intercede, and never think that it must be exactly the way some other person or group have found helpful. Probably each of us has an individual gift which he wants us to use. I always hope, for instance, that when I am meditating in his presence on the books I try to write, and while I am asking to understand what he wants me to learn from himself and to share with others, that those thoughts and meditations do also go forth in some way, and perhaps reach other minds and suggest new ideas.

I have been so happy and encouraged to receive letters from more than one friend to whom I sent this little book, *God's Transmitters*, saying, "Just recently I found myself thinking very much along the same lines, and now wonder if some of your thoughts had reached me." I am certain, in my own case, that those of you who pray for me have been used again and again in this way, transmitting to my mind some of our Lord's thoughts, more often and more beautifully than you or I can understand.